William Moore

Nocturnes and other Poems

William Moore

Nocturnes and other Poems

ISBN/EAN: 9783337397890

Printed in Europe, USA, Canada, Australia, Japan

Cover: Foto ©Andreas Hilbeck / pixelio.de

More available books at **www.hansebooks.com**

NOCTURNES

AND OTHER POEMS.

BY

REV. W. MOORE,

AUTHOR OF

'A HARP FROM THE WILLOWS,' 'LOST CHORDS'

LONDON :

ELLIOT STOCK, 62, PATERNOSTER ROW, E.C.

1898.

CONTENTS

An Excursion

898—1898

O VIEWLESS dove, who waftest oft
   From all the landscape pale,
Enwrapt beneath thy pinions soft,
   Quick tidings of the vale,

Some knell, too drowsy for alarm,
   Along this summer dark,
Or cackle of the dreaming farm,
   Or watchdog's sudden bark;

Thou journeyest over woodlands brown
   From all the glimmering hills;
And there I know an ancient down
   The southern welkin fills;

But land mists, shot with silvery beams,
    And azure of the night
Awhile have veiled it, ere it gleams
    In its own chalky white.

O breeze, that wistest living things
    So swiftly and so well!
Naught hast thou in thy whisperings
    Of yon great hill to tell?

When quivering died the sunset flames
    Downward, thou camest so
To fan the rushes of the Thames
    A thousand years ago.

Ah! thou art weak, and hidden there
    Lie memories of death,
Of beacon fires, and battle blare,
    Too clamorous for thy breath.

One comes—her brows are gemmed with light—
    Who is she, whose strong car
Shall on the storied slopes to-night
    Climb where the ancients are?

Not History : she cannot move
    A mistress on that way.
Not Fancy : for, content to rove,
    She drives her steeds astray.

But one she is who fares full well
    With second-sighted eyes ;
Casts on the path her rainbow light,
    Yet sees realities.

Men call her, if a name be aught,
    Imagination now :
Yet once no other Pindar brought
    To Castaly's green brow.

Forward o'er lea and stream and wood !
    Her lightning-pacèd steeds
Shall show where British Muses stood,
    And legends turned to deeds.

Already on the darkened wold !
    Just hushed, o'er yonder plain,
A thousand springs now backward rolled,
    The war-cry of the Dane !

An Excursion

How thick and far the woodlands lie,
　　How their dark fringes creep,
Black-crested waves of greenery,
　　To hollows of this steep!

Yet here and there a Saxon light
　　Is glimmering on the fell,
Where some rude-timbered tower in sight
　　Has stilled its vesper bell;

There, freed at last by Alfred's bond,
　　The carl is on his bed;
There, Alfred's holy horn-book conned,
　　Rests many a flaxen head.

Young spirits resolute to pore
　　O'er lessons on that page
Which deeper sink than all the lore
　　Taught in this newer age.

And haply, too, their sleeping sire
　　Hath hands that grasp the plough,
The scythe, the flail, with cheerier fire
　　Than hands which grasp them now.

" Thou art not here to moralize
  On good that is or was;
But turn and read, with opened eyes,
  This record on the grass."

So spake my Guide, and ill restrained
  Her steeds, impatient still :
Her sister witch had sudden rained
  A glory o'er the hill.

And lo ! a horse, in outline pale
  Against the western slope,
Spreads a vast flank and world of tail,
  And upward to the cope

Rears an outlandish neck or mane,
  And head of artless round ;
And prancing seems to paw the inane
  Above a gulf profound,

Where the west sides in channels deep
  And swathes abrupt descend,
And the green pillars of the steep
  In clustered darkness end.

But lo! to northward, where it turns
   A gentler slope again,
With hinder feet the monster spurns
   A little thorn-set plain ;

And, where the bushes thickest are,
   White with its chalky seams
And gashed with many a moonlit scar,
   A hillock ghost-like gleams :

Pendragon's hill, the mound of kings !
   What bones of Britain's best,
What names that woke the bardic strings,
   In its dim chambers rest !

And springing from the ancient tomb
   The horse yet seems to stay,
As angel over catacomb,
   To bear some soul away.

O let not prying History come
   To tear that mystic horse
From its own place and proper home
   By Arthur's royal corse.

Where dying in the ranks of war
  He shed the Saxon blood.
Avalon surely is not far,
  Nor far its ambient flood.

To-night at Wantage Alfred sleeps
  After his long day's toil ;
His draughtsmen never on these steeps
  For trophy trenched the soil.

His victory rang away to east,
  Beyond yon hazy hill :
And since this giant first was cast
  'Tis three fierce centuries still.

" Wilt thou, then, measure hence," she says
  (My Guide, who reins the car),
" One more millennial of days,
  Now thou hast fared so far ?

" Thine ears shall drink the harpers' dirge
  O'er Arthur's funeral.
Forward ! Four scarlet legions surge
  At dawn through yonder val :

" Their blazing camp-fires brown the sward
  And solitary firs
Of cromlech groves, which seer nor bard,
  Naught but the night breeze stirs.

" They march to the rebellious Usk,
  Their moving column dread
Shall scare the bosky plains till dusk
  With clangours of their tread.

" Forward!   For me 'tis e'er the same,
  To reach the founts of time.
I'll show thee forms, ere Julius came,
  Gay in a misty clime :

And white-robed gazers on the stars
  Fix days of fight and fate ;
And warriors blue and scythèd cars
  Pour through yon grassy gate.

" Forward ; e'en yet another race,
  Another garb is now :
Two mount, midsummer morn, to face
  The orient crimson glow ;

" To hail their god in all his power :
　　They know their calendar.
'Tis graven on the stones which tower
　　On that strange plain afar

" Where flinty portals ever span
　　The changeless solstices,
And all the circling cloisters scan
　　Heaven's starry mysteries.

" E'en now the flame-robed priesthoods sweep
　　Down that well-meted way
Which points where on the verge shall peep
　　The golden eye of Day."

" Ah, Lady ! leave me," I replied ;
　　" With undistracted gaze
Let others quickened at thy side
　　See sights of dateless days :

" But let me on this hill of death,
　　Though sweet its dirges call,
Think Alfred's England lies beneath
　　And see that acorn fall

" From his strong hand, which steadfast grew
    Amidst a stormful world,
The oak whose leaves and giant thew
    A thousand springs unfurled.

" See ! on his woods the night-wind dies,
    The tides of twilight creep,
And rings of curling azure rise
    From all the dusky deep.

" Already o'er his Oxenford
    Day in thin radiant fires
Is bringing heaven's revealing word
    To light his five dark shires.

" And where to northward all the vale
    To yon dark edge is rolled,
The beechland tops e'en now are pale,
    Tipped with the herald gold :

" And from his guardian stream uplifts
    The darkness fast, to tell
Where weirs are murmuring, and down drifts
    The loaded coracle.

" 'Tis morn." Nor blanched she at the sight,
  Nor hailed her inward eye
That broad sun less than mystic night
  And moon's soft witchery.

And now she showed, as something loved,
  All the long Saxon day
And toil which the slow oxen moved,
  Or in the woodland lay.

But chiefly beyond Cumnor hirst,
  Where Frideswide's belfries ring
And some meek scholars quench their thirst
  At learning's baby spring;

Where Ina's code, and lore of Bede
  Light up their later age;
And all the former things they read
  On God's more cherished page;

And still for them fierce echoes come
  From Mercia's conscious hills;
And sainted Edmund's martyrdom
  The living memory fills;

How heathen captors bent their bow,
    Their arrows ready made
In heathen quivers, to lay low
    That kingly perfect head.

Ah! better bitter herbs and crust
    Of lore, with love's sweet smile,
Than, with faith's heart all turned to dust,
    Stalled ox and sugar'd pile.

Better their oaken chantries dim,
    With storm-stained horny pane,
Than spires and pictured seraphim
    In creedless college fane.

Then, as to pluck some pearl again
    From Time's far ocean deep,
Her wand swept o'er the Benoc's plain,
    And woke from secular sleep

Some day of glory—not that rang
    (I asked her not for these)
With deeds of battle; but that sang
    The ancient Pascal peace,

When all the dark fritillaries flash
   On Isis' breathing sides
In balmier light : and where the ash
   And mossy copse-floor hides

The tormentil's rathe tiny head,
   Creeps Heaven's unstinted gold :
" So on the poor God's wage," she said,
   " Pours after Winter's cold."

"Their wage!" I said. "Yes! thou couldst draw,
   And, Lady, thou alone,
Their annals thence : though never law,
   Nor e'er one carven stone,

" Nor tomb, nor rude memorial
   Knew them, nor civic change
Writ on the hall or castle wall,
   Or keep or moated grange,

" Their wages still the tale could tell,
   And figures touched by thee
Would make no barren chronicle,
   But living pageant be.

" Oh, show how slaved, how fared those hands
    Which lopped each ashen glade ;
Or tamed yon ragwort-breeding lands,
    And all an Eden made."

" Alas ! thou askest to thy grief,"
    She said ; " I should reveal
Dire Winter after Summer brief,
    And still for them to feel.

" Yet list awhile : from that strange lore
    Four pictures shall display
The long declension of the poor
    E'en to their modern day.

" The barons' battles flash afar,
    And Severn runs with blood :
Yet ne'er did that familiar war
    Make scarce the poor man's food.

" Ah ! Plenty's smile !   Ah ! Summer days !
    The mendicants of God
Cried, as their Francis, on yon ways
    And wastes they barefoot trod :

" ' Give all, who can : to give is heaven :'
   Rich, then, were all the pence ;
And freely, hourly, boon was given
   From hospital and spence.

" Next comes Reform, like Autumn frost ;
   The poor man's friends are gone ;
His very guild lands all are lost ;
   For eggs they give a stone :

" For Law, with the collection plate,
   And priests may beat the doors
Of hearts of lords now satiate
   With all the convent stores.

" But, when they wrench the niggard dole,
   'Tis silver's base alloy ;
Base as the plunderer and his soul,
   That, giving, knows no joy.

" Next Newbury sees leal Falkland fall ;
   Cromwellian pikes are strong :
But did trained bands and yeomen all
   Avenge one rural wrong ?

" Was Oxford leaguered to restore
  To his lost green again,
To common land or fuel store,
  One peasant of yon plain ?

" Rather they ride from shop, from farm
  To mar the sanctuary
Of her who still could pour the balm
  On voiceless poverty.

" And last, when France, by hunger-pain,
  Infuriate, shook the yoke,
And most on yonder very plain,
  The grim starvation spoke,

" Not with her nameless butcheries,
  With words farouche and wild
Only in sad and famished eyes
  Of paling, phthisic child.

" The justice (God the title save !)
  Fixed down meek Labour's wage :
But not the price of Life's poor stave—
  That 'scaped his iron gauge.

" And then came war's fierce cup to drink,
  And flood of twelvemonth rains,
But sacred land rents must not shrink,
  Nor eke the farmer's gains.

" So, landlord, look! Thine acres feed
  Still one superfluous slave:
Ah! send him, as a useless weed,
  To the Union's living grave.

" Yes! From the fields his grandsires tilled,
  And made so rich for thee,
Drive him. By others be fulfilled
  The debt to misery."

" And now," I cried, " how ends this plight,
  And what to-morrow's chance?"
(But she had vanished with the light
  Of her fair countenance.)

" But not for thee so ends the tale,
  Hill! that hast roused to arms
With beacon-fires the slumbering Vale
  Oft against heathen swarms.

" Let others, round thy viewless hearth
　　Rallying for refuge, seek,
Amidst Time's heathenish wrongs, the earth
　　Which still awaits the meek.

" Let oft in summer toiling wight
　　Descry thine outline dim
High floating in the liquid light
　　And whispering joy to him;

" Then, as the thronging breezes bring
　　Thy memories of the brave,
He'll bless afar a patriot king,
　　He'll hail a hero's grave."

In the Swift Night of Old

HER towers are bright beneath the moon;
High fleecy clouds seem stretched upon
The pinnacles, or torn and rent
To creep through one arched battlement,
Lacing its gray with silver thread.
The golden stars are overhead,
Their eyes on murmuring Itchen, save
Where bending laurels quaff the wave.
Many a night serene as this
Hath poured the balm of midnight bliss
On Wykeham's towers; e'en such a night
Bathed walls new-chiselled in the light,

2 -2

In the Swift Night of Old

Ending that day when busier halls
From idlesse of proud castle walls
Gathered the best of Albion
In Learning's newer race to run.

Night loses not : through flowers of fire
Her dusky coursers never tire
To strain the fresh aerial thew
Up all the slopes of misted blue.
And, as she mounts, her starlit eyes
Gaze on the youngest galaxies,
On orbs, far-flaming, infinite,
Sown in the immeasurable height ;
And life is in that dust of gold
Glittering untarnished as of old.
And then she bends to look below.
The streams by darkened chambers flow.
Here, too, she finds the gift is given,
The gift not alien from her heaven ;
Here, too, there sleeps eternal youth
Amidst firm bulwarks of the truth :

Sleeps but to wake these courts among,
To sport, to labour, and to song,
Each morn renewing every bliss :
And now upon these walls her kiss,
Serenest, closest, warmest, clings :
For here, amongst all lower things,
An endless line, replenished ever,
As fountains feed a rushing river,
Lives on with youth's bright energies
Most like her own.   It never dies,
The scholar line, the hero brood,
Close linked in holy brotherhood.

Hark ! from her car the Genius falls
On carven roofs and shadowy walls.
His wings, as of an angel, over
The courts, the scalèd gardens, hover.
He sings a past and future story.
But mortal yet ne'er knew the glory
Of all the record : for he tells
Things written in no chronicles

By human hands on parchment dim ;
For sun ne'er rose unwatched by him :
He heard, as oft the crimson ray,
Bright usher of some festal day,
Melted the dense unfolding cloud
On Catherine's mountain, from the crowd
In silver peals the clarions fling
Their welcome to a youthful king,
Fair Richard, or that holier head
Back to his nursing mother led
From lilied Tamise.   He doth know
All the still nights in chambers low ;
How oft the quivering moonbeams played
On oaken floors, and boyhood laid
In slumber.   On the novice' sight
He spread that dream where falcons bright
No more should mount in storm-swift flight
O'er forest glades, nor cherished steed
Should turn, beseeching to be fed :
Nor Summer from the well-known hills
Toss all his garden daffodils.

Another spell is on him now :
The gleaming of a mitred brow,
The silver of a vesper bell,
The shrines ablaze, the organ's swell :
And daily in a grander hall
Full many a gray-haired seneschal
Marshals the equal feast, and he,
Heir of a new nobility,
Sits at the board, in sable fold
Of robe that never shall grow old,
The scholar's gown : no more a page
Mocking the gaudy thriftless age
In sammit.   Then new voices seem
To change the glory of his dream :
And call him to the new crusades
Where young knights grasp new battle-blades,
The spirit's sword—and still they cry
" Down with the feudal tyranny !
Be thou not slack.   Abundant now
For thee the living fountains flow
Where kings and prelates guard thee round
As nursing sires."   The Ave's sound

In the Swift Night of Old

Is mingled with the notes of morn.
He wakes, and on the gates of horn
The Genius turns his shadowy key :
The rest to come he may not see.

Four Years After

I.

Down the hillside to the Abbey forest leaves are
    falling now ;
But like yellow domes of foliage elms unruined tower
    below.

Round them, rolling from the valley, vapour of late
    autumn creeps,
Ghost of breezes that in May-time thrilled them to
    their greenest deeps ;

Rolling, show the peopled background, all the flooded
    waste along ;
Spires and cupolas and turrets, fanes and halls, a
    mystic throng.

Ah ! the leaves of love and leisure, faith and hope,
    are yellow there :
Or these eyes see all things fading, jaundiced with
    a quick despair.

Four years since upon this upland with a new-found
    friend I stood :
Such a misty eve of autumn gloomed the city,
    drenched the wood.

Yet for us hope's magic rainbow all a glittering
    landscape spanned ;
We were standing on our Pisgah, gazing on a pro-
    mised land.

Every spire now pointing yonder pointed to a vault
    divine ;
Every garden was an Eden, every cloister was a
    shrine.

Paths and avenues long trodden by pale masters of
    the soul
Still must lead, who loyal follow, to the self-same
    golden goal.

Sophia beckoned with no seeming treachery in her
    lovely smile ;
Coral bells of baby Science, could they e'er to ill
    beguile ?

Yes, the ribbons flutter gaily, sunlit, on the raw
    recruits ;
Gay their banner floats above them, waving o'er
    their joyous flutes !

But 'tis sombre, rent and riddled, on the smoking
    battleground ;
When the sod is stained around it ; stained from
    many a mortal wound.

Oxford calls the flower of England, all she wants of
    heart and brain ;
Banners of her past and present yearly herald her
    campaign.

Then the drill, the drum, the muster ;—but, behold,
    an ambuscade !
Now to eyes of hundreds dying all the flaunting
    glories fade !

II.

Ah, they say, speak not for others: thou art a
   degenerate son ;
Worse than useless thy complaining : see, thy
   Mother marches on.

Well, then, only for one wounded will I here con-
   fession make ;
Here where mournful tears of evening trickle from
   the darkening brake ;

One pale golden gleam of sunset, lamplike on the
   wooded hill,
Guards the cloud-enwoven curtain, where One ear is
   listening still :

Not as where all ears are listening for some new
   thing to be told ;
And the temptress tongue is bid for, and in yonder
   Athens sold.

Search, Diogenes, the gardens, search the book-
lined chambers all :
Is there one shall speak God's comfort in a true
confessional ?

No, belated little robin, warbling in the oaken
grove,
Thou art better sign of comfort, holier teacher of
God's love.

But alas ! long since they called us from the Father's
birds and flowers ;
" Seek true loveliness with Plato, seek it in eternal
bowers."

There around their Things all real, Beauty, Good-
ness, Truth, we trod ;
Wandering waited, waited wondering, where amongst
them all was God.

Sudden cried from dark abysses voices of another
crew :*
" Fancies these ! Avaunt ! let logic lead you to a
Substance true."

* Spinoza's followers.

"Forward to a goal receding! forward to the
    Infinite!"—
Though the heart and soul be outraged, starved,
    and deadened in the flight.

Soul! long since the Stagyrite robbed her of her
    grace in life or death ;
Function doomed of dying body, as in broken flutes
    the breath.

On with mind to grasp the utmost;--though creation
    lie between ;
And revealing words long spoken, and revealing
    deeds have been.

Doubt, the darkened heart's blank twilight, all that
    central prospect mars ;
Dims the spirit's sweetest colours, takes their bright-
    ness from her stars.

" What!" they cry, "no wings to follow, old-world
    moorings cast away!
Fall, then, fall, thou less than Phaethon, ere thou
    seest the coming day !"

III.

So once more earth's green things round us : but
    that fire has singed the hair,
Furnace fire has passed upon us : One to quench it
    was not there.

For such souls to earth returning, to its scenes and
    duties clear,
Find them other than they loved them ere they went
    their mad career.

With faith waning, wanes the Conscience ; garbling
    all her simple rule,
Still utility will oust her, echo of a creedless school.

City, to whose fanes are wending they who own no
    Saviour's name,
They whose Law, long work of Reason, never from
    the Mountain came ;

In whose halls are many merchants trafficking in all
    things fair,
Slaves, and souls of men, and gold-set gems of
    thought, delicious ware;

Babylon, mystery, art thou fallen? yet I will not
    wish thee woe,
Not for all the hopes thou killest, cherished fifty
    months ago.

IV.

Rather let a modern snow melt into some former
    joy:
Pearl of pearls thou wast, for all his student days, to
    many a boy.

Often, on this happy hilltop, sons of prophets stood
    to gaze;
Often on a morn of summer thou wert glorious in
    the haze;

When its mists like waves of silver into coasts of
    purple rolled,
Eastwards in thy guardian uplands drenching many
    a wooded fold,

And along the verdant valley, as to thronèd queen
    her slaves,
Streams in sunlight ran to meet thee, rivers reached
    their vassal waves,

Down to belfries, oriel chambers, havens in a realm's
    distress,
Vaulted vistas, sealèd gardens, nooks of peace and
    plenteousness.

But in all those happy mornings, whose have been
    the happiest eyes,
Hailing hence thy truest grandeur, counting best thy
    destinies ?

Looked they when the child of Gerald* wandered to
    thy halls, and went,
Leaving lamps of wisdom lit in many a long-locked
    muniment ;

         * Erasmus.

Left a radiance on dim pages giant libraries among,
Left his golden key that opens all the founts of
　　Grecia's song ?

Rather, when from chairs and pulpits loud the white
　　Dominican
Christward bent all heathen thinking, every treasured
　　thought of man ;

When in humbler cell or hostel voiceless hearts to
　　heaven aspired,
Meek as Origen, yet with ardours wiser than of
　　Plato fired ;

When from yonder ivied Abbey matin chants awoke
　　the birds,
When the vesper call of Godstow floated Thames-
　　ward to the herds.

Better that than modern comforts, hushed the
　　orison, fallen the bell ;
Unctions to souls unbelieving, how we know, we
　　reason well !

V.

Scorner of the hands that built thee, where are
    Faith's entrusted flowers?
Pining for the air that oped them!   Stamped to clay
    beneath thy towers!

Yet farewell; I will not curse thee.   One nobility
    is thine,
One coal living from the altar, one ray stolen from
    the shrine.

Over flesh thou hast dominion; on the adder thou
    dost go;
Though thy heaven is cold and Christless, thy
    regards are not below.

So beneath the stars of Egypt, zeal, for which
    Hypatia died,
By one holy cord of continence to the Nazarene's
    was allied.

Nor shall e'er thy lodger Science, with her gases
and her knife,
Teach thee shifting sands of senses build man's
intellectual life.

Thus austere, thy poet loved once: in his faultless
singing meet
All the rigours of thy thinking, all that chasteness
gives of sweet.

Loved he too thy wolds and rivers; and to the
olden watershed
Came one moonlit eve of autumn—came to mourn
his Thyrsis dead.

And the magic of thy copses, listing thy eternal
chimes,
And thy swain,* on slopes of summer clearly fluting,
filled her rhymes.

But the dirge of Dorian waters closes the enchanting
song;
Nevermore his brother singeth who to Nature must
belong.

                    * A. H. Clough.

VI.

So by pagan paths thou leadest to thy double goals
    on high!
Light, that oft must turn to darkness; sweetness,
    into apathy;

So on virgin snows of Reason, and along her
    dazzling horns,
Fare thy gifted ones : but sudden Doubt's sheer gulf
    before them yawns.

While beneath them in her valley Faith still keeps
    the scornèd hearth;
And her gaze can fix still heavenward, though her
    steps are on the earth.

Light and Dark in Spring

I.

'Tis vain a sorrow here to find,
Or sighing in this balmy wind
O'er Nature rising fresh and kind.

With all her eyes she is awake:
Anemones their whiteness make
Beneath the purple-budding brake:

And, like a vein of bounding blood,
Her brooklet at its tiny flood,
Threading lush mazes of the wood,

Wends out to meadow waterways
Amidst her hyacinths' blue haze
And all the marigolds ablaze.

II.

No darkness comes upon the noon,
Such as in lost Judæa's swoon
And Satan's hour was poured upon

The shimmering olives on the hill,
And gloomed the foaming of the rill,
And made each plumaged warbler still.

But in yon copse each tufted tree
Like green crest on a sunlit sea
Joins the gay tumult, blest and free.

No symbol sad of sin and care,
No crosses three are outlined there
Athwart the boon unclouded air.

The golden catkins are aglow :
But will their rifled tassels show
That scene of triumph changed to woe

When waving palms by palms were met,
And all the singers' tide was set
Down the strewn slope of Olivet ?

Light and Dark in Spring

Bright on yon spire shines chanticleer :
Strange emblem of a dawning drear
And clangour mocking Peter's fear.

I hear the lark's wild ecstasy
Lost in high azures of the sky :
But no exceeding bitter cry.

Nor e'en yon robin's russet breast
To Calvary's tree was ever prest ;
For Nature's festival he's drest.

III.

Ah, fields ! ah, seas of bursting green !
Have ye forgotten what hath been
To win your joyous look serene ?

Or is it that Man's heart hath found
Oblivion in this splendour round,
And in your peace all remorse drowned ?

This Love transfusing wintry gleams,
Which on the bush an incense seems
And living breath upon the streams,

Can it portray the Love that wore
Our flesh and every burden bore,
Till iron and the death-swoon tore

Body from soul; and downward bent
Blenched lips which to the firmament
Their cry of dereliction sent?

Doth Man still recreant grasp the bliss
Which wooes him on a morn like this,
And yet the Son doth never kiss?

IV.

Wherefore rejoice?   Yon spire doth rise,
But pagan manner hardly dies;
The little world in bondage lies.

The farmer strides the laughing lea
Unshriven as the innocent tree;
In sooth he is no Pharisee.

Or if to him aught mystic come,
'Tis some dim touch of heathendom;
It chases far the Gospel gloom.

Light and Dark in Spring

The April sun has dashed the tears
From Ostria's cheek : and why should fears
Or sorrow mar the look she wears ?

Balder was dead : but now in white
He lives again in floods of light :
And Odin gladdens at the sight.

These hearts are fat as brawn within ;
And who shall there an entrance win
With any whispers of earth's sin ?

For them no change their Easter brings
Save the brute movement of the springs :
The oak is cased with annual rings

On growths of comfortable years ;
And knells of Passiontide fall on ears
Quite void of mediæval fears ;

Nor wake within a noble pain
Midst darling hates, and thoughts that stain,
And thick thorns choking unseen grain

While earth's increase they mark so well,
And all her greening blades can tell
And how her fifty-folds will sell,

While their strong hind the harrow lifts,
And all the gathered grossness sifts
To fuse it on his smoking drifts.

But sordid aims shall never tire:
And sturdy sins to son from sire
Live on beneath the rural spire.

And souls are burdened still, and bound
In Nature's simple painless round
Still balmless for their cancerous wound.

V.

Yet see, one crawls afield : no gains
Hath Earth for him : but only pains,
The heritage of winter rains.

Away the veteran hand they fling;
Without him from the genial spring
Their cautious profits now they wring.

And all the almoners of the poor
Have fled yon Priory : now Christ's store
Is locked behind the Union door.

And so he locks his heart to love
And God's own dying to remove
A long-stored vengeance from above.

He hears not in the Passion song
A vengeance on one rural wrong :
It doth the suffering still prolong !

VI.

Yes ! yes ! an evil festers still ;
For all the living airs that fill
Yon copses on the morning hill.

And yet up Golgotha's dark stair
A breeze most magic, yet most fair,
Shall meet each mourner mounting there ;

And flood him, as with cleansing tide,
Wafted from where Apollyon died
Beneath a Saviour's wounded side ;

Where flashed in gloom the avenging knife
And cut the canker eating life,
The greed, the pride, the sin, the strife,

And once again man's life-blood gushed,
And all his soul with health was flushed,
And all his heart in love was hushed.

Nicias and a Sequel

O'ER Athens' columned citadels
And green Arcadia's shepherd dells,
O'er Sparta's rock-encircled valley,
And white sails of the bounding galley
That slowly breaks the Ionian foam,
Straining for Hellas and for home,
The Dawn is coming: on the flow
Of Western waves she reddens now,
And bursting upon Sicily,
Her trembling purple floods the sky:
But, untouched by her rosy fingers,
On each dark hill the night-cloud lingers;
Nor yet the rocks, where dews are streaming,
Upon the precipice are gleaming;

Nor yet the pines—with sombre dress
Covering the craggy wilderness,
Where never climber dare intrude
On Ætna's fiery solitude—
Pierce through the mist's enfolding cloud
With one spire of their tufted crowd:
Only from out the gray profound
Is heard afar the cataract's sound,
As rushing from its airy steep
Onward it dashes to the deep.
But, see! before advancing Day
The morning mists have rolled away;
And colours from that magic beam
Flash out upon the winding stream,
And woods in untamed majesty
Toss their bright foliage to the sky,
Where, clear above the unnumbered throng,
Sweet Philomel begins her song.

But can the light on wood and river
Rekindle hopes now quenched for ever?

The tears that blind the Athenian's eye—
Can they take pleasure from yon sky?
Or loves he now the sparkling wave
That rolls above his comrade's grave,
And drifts toward the death-strewn shore
Each shattered trireme, mast, and oar,
And bursts in idly-foaming spray
Far at the entrance to the bay,
Where the chained galleys, firm and high,
Deny him flight and liberty?
From Syracuse a sound is sent,
And turret, dome, and battlement,
Are ringing with the exulting cry
Of pæan-chanting victory:
And beacon-fires are smouldering still
On Euryalus' castled hill,
And high upon Plemmyrium
Bid the Sicilian armies come,
To view the last expiring throe
Of their thrice-baffled captive foe;
And from each inward-gazing glen
The dread alarm of coming men

Sounds o'er the marsh, where, silently,
Anapus wanders to the sea ;
Or seems to sound : each airy breath
To that doomed army whispers death.

Despair has hushed the piercing cry
That rose from thousands to the sky,
When Syracuse, but yesterday,
With one clear pæan swept the bay,
And forward o'er the drowned and dying
Pressed on their ranks in panic flying
As leaves of Autumn, pale and sere,
Are crowded on the wind-swept mere.
And he stands there whom Athens sent
To be the unwilling instrument
Of her ambition's wildest deed :
Whose warning voice she would not heed.
But what if years of fight and storm
And pain have marred his wasted form,
Pain that his country, heeding not,
Still bound him to the soldier's lot ?

And what if power and fame be fled ?
High Duty's laws are never dead.
Lit by a flame within the heart,
They brighten, never to depart.
'Tis Athens still that fills his sight,
And breathes within the undaunted might
To save the remnant of her host :
While life remains, not all is lost.

And now another morning shines
Upon their long retreating lines,
And loud the wail is heard again
From the death-cumbered shore and plain.
Onward, with unaverted eyes,
They pass, where in the gateway lies
The abandoned crowd : they must not see
That last despairing agony ;
Though oft a son's or father's groan
Is heard in answer to their own.
But others, with last hope still strong,
Are following wistfully along ;

Some to their once-loved comrade clinging,
Round his dear neck their arms are flinging,
And wildly calling on their love
With cries and tears that may not move,
Till, feebly sinking in despair,
They pour to heaven their latest prayer.

The last farewell is over now,
And they move forward, mute and slow.
But ever memory recalls
That voyage from Athens' clamorous walls,
And hopes that grasped in victory
All treasures of the Western sea ;
And then the days which cast their brave
To welter on the harbour wave ;
Or, slain in fight, no burial given,
To lie beneath the unpitying heaven.
And last, the flight from that dread shore
To ills perhaps unknown before,
O'erpowers them : and the starting tear
Speaks of the woes too hard to bear.

But Nicias' voice is ever by
To cheer their deep despondency.
" For ills ye cannot now retrieve,
Forbear, my countrymen, to grieve!
Forbear the unavailing tear
For those beyond the reach of fear!
The wings of Nemesis, which over
The invading squadron darkly hover,
Are soaring now, for she has spent
Her last wrath on our armament,
And bears to the Olympian king
The tribute of long suffering;
Nor can the offended Power deny
To humbled hearts security.
Look on yourselves; and chase Despair
From out those ranks still firm and fair
With discipline; where'er ye go,
A city terrifies the foe,
Which towers can never fortify
As the brave soul and spirit high.
E'en now from off her unmanned walls
Your own Athene loudly calls

Across the intervening main
Her sons and city back again.
Her breathing sons! her own dear band,
She calls, the active heart and hand—
And not the hulks that strew yon strand!
Oh! live to join her choral throng;
Strike for the sunny land of song.
Some eve on well-remembered wave
Mute for their welcome, shall our brave
See sunset from Cithæron glance
In glory on Our Lady's lance?"

*   *   *   *

Who stifled that heroic breath?
Whose hand did mix that cup of death,
Drained in the dungeon-house, to sate
Sicilia's triumphant hate?
'Twas Syracuse that bid him die,
Where oft for highest minstrelsy
His laureate harp had Pindar strung,
And oft the banquet-halls had rung
Loud with the song-inspirèd grace
That told of Hiero's swift race,

And welcomed in the enduring lay
The victor of the bloodless bay.
But none of Hellas' bards e'er shed
The light of song on Nicias' head,
Or let one tuneful teardrop fall
Upon his nameless funeral.
To captive wretch what song is meet?
Who sings to chronicle defeat?
Enough for him unknown to lie,
And silence hymn his victory.

So, not upon the curtained scene,
Melpomene, tear-compelling queen,
Not only on thine Attic board
Is terror woke, and pity poured.
While there thy mimics wear the mask
Of greatness, and the hero's task,
Thou treadest then on purple seas,
Thou showest fate on asphodel leas;
Thou teachest e'en amidst the smile
Of some wave-kissed Levantine isle

How o'er a nation broods the storm,
And the bolt scathes one innocent form.

But waft me back thy rocks among,
The bulwarks of thy land of song;
Though now for all its chivalry
It feeds alone the wandering bee;
Though now alone the nibbling sheep
Hang o'er its white and marble steep,
And wide and far proud Sparta rides
On all the blue Ægean tides.
Yonder by Argolis' twinkling strand
Her triremes move. Ah, wave thy wand!
And blot them in thy shifting scene;
Let modern wonders come between—
Already! all the banks of oars
Melt to a mass of moving towers,
The flashes of the hoplites' glaive
To mouths that menace all the wave
Opening from monstrous glittering throats
On giant decks. Ah! whither floats

Yon squadron, leaving vapours black
O'er the white whirlpools of its track?

Again for Athens! ruthless queen!
Again for Athens, what hath been!
Nay, forces of a fiercer age
Thou gatherest on the watery stage.
Is this thy newest tragedy
Amidst the islands of the sea,
For her who, since her brave went down
Around the bitter Dorian town,
E'en when a sterner storm of fate
Her docks, her streets, made desolate,
The Crescent hovering o'er the blue,
Never, to Wisdom being true,
Suffered that earth-born withering glow
Her mind and spirit to lay low?
For she had passed with smile divine
From Plato's walk to Christ's own shrine.
In vain—when the overwhelming hoard
Their false book brandished and a sword

Blood-purpled from Byzantium
And many a violated home,
And thundered round her convent walls,
And with their jargon filled her halls—
In vain their hornèd symbol shone
Upon her matchless Parthenon.

Again that front of marble pale
Has felt the kiss of Freedom's gale.
And never in morn's crimson flush
That snow seemed melted to a blush
More lovely, than on that bright day
When to the quays, the docks, the bay,
From every hill a nation sped
To see its chosen legions tread
On gallant transports, ere they loose
The hawsers for no Syracuse,
But where the heights of Candia mourn
For saints that bleed and shrines that burn.
Hark! how along each high-hung shroud
The Britons cheer: their pæan loud

Is answered by Italia's sons
From all their steel-clad galleons :
A prince upon the gangway goes ;
The sword is bared on Europe's foes.

So hopes are high, and hearts are light ;
Thy preludes ever end aright.
Still on thy ringing plains of Troy
Thou show'st the brief delirious joy :
But then thou callest men to list
Thy fallen great protagonist,
Him who from Salamis came in ships,
In accents taught by thy pale lips,
Ere from his side the bursting shower
Shall feed the purple-blooming flower,
Upon the grassy stage complain
That the fast friend doth not remain.
Yes, pennons there, once friendly, fly
Of England and of Italy.
They speed to join the stern conclave
Stretched many a league along the wave ;

To threat with iron panoply
The peasant struggling to be free ;
And Greece is landing on that shore
Gifts to a modern Minotaur,
Till she, to fate no longer blind,
But waking from her dream, shall find
A prison or a nameless grave
In that sad isle she came to save.

But hark ! a fiercer tumult drowns
The bitter cry of Candia's towns.
From lands late won from Anarchy's curse
The messengers of new reverse
Tell where a spreading panic fills
The folds of all the slanting hills.
Methinks 'twas there one pipe could tame
The dappled lynxes ; and they came
And couched with lambkins : and from dens
Far in the green Othrysian glens
A tawny squadron leonine
Marched—for the lilting was divine ;

And from the cone-strewn coverts drawn
E'en the light ankles of the fawn
Bold on the sunny slopes advance
To join the rapturous jocund dance.
Now pealing through a lurid night
The trumpets urge to wilder flight
Steeds riderless, and the human stream,
Oft lit with sudden sulphur gleam,
The routed men, the women weeping :
While o'er the harvests ripe are sweeping
The turbaned foe, a myriad hoofs ;
Afar abandoned burning roofs
Fringe the dark plain with tongues of flame ;
With quivering tongues that tell the shame
How Hellas never kept the gate
That stemmed right well the flood of fate.
Ah ! vantage ground divine was hers
O'er Tempe's rocks, in Pelion's firs :
And oft had she amidst the shade
Of all those giant gorges made
Full on the foe her lightnings flash,
And by the stream her thunders crash :

And from her fastnesses rushing down
Confusion on the invader thrown.
Wherefore that sudden panic flight
When stars were conscious, till morn's light
Blushed on a scene of camp-fires dead,
Dismantled hold, and warrior fled?
Now in this silence of sheathed swords
What strain can fit, what choric words?
Ah! better end thy tragedy
Amidst those islands of the sea.

The Life of S. Augustine

THE keels that broke all day the Tuscan foam
This eve pass swiftly to their glassy home ;
There in their forests on old Tiber's tide
The merchant masts of many a kingdom ride ;
And pennons fluttering in the golden skies
Tell what fair climes have sent those argosies :
While on the quays a thousand traders pour
Their sunny wines, their harvests, and their ore.

Here laurelled leaders oft, here seamen stood
By Glory hailed from some far scene of blood.
And yet to-night beyond yon garden wall
Two victors sit more noble than them all ;
Two brows now brightening with a triumph given,
Two souls now anchored in the port of heaven :

Although no curious crowd might choose to come
Beneath their casement in the gathering gloom ;
Nor speech, nor language in the listening air
Tells of the joy that brings and binds them there.

Soon shall be writ for ever, but not now,
The story of his early-furrowed brow :
His eyes now chastened with a new-found grace
That tames the eagle contour of his face :
His lips now parted in expectancy
Of some dim answer from beyond the sky :
And the dark ardours of his cheek, whose blood
Beats to new touches of infinitude.
Her story, too, who here, hand clasped in hand,
Mounts with his spirit to a heavenly land ;
Companion pure, who aids him in his flight ;
Soars, as he soars, towards the eternal light,
With the pale glory of her patient eyes
Lit with the fire of love's long sacrifice :
Fire that on lips of her who never faints
Wreathes incense given to the prayers of saints.

So he is saved at last : but oft she wept,
E'en when this darling in his cradle slept ;
In that wild land would yet a pagan's smile
From the straight narrow way his faith beguile ?
Or Pride deflower him when he wore the gown
In the gay license of some Christless town ;
Nor yet the washing of the heavenly dew
On that young soul might come to make it new,
Lest the blest seal, by some dark sin effaced,
On branded brow might never be replaced ?

Or when his boyhood, as a flower in light,
Oped blooms beyond thine expectation bright,
Was it all joy, blest soul, or was it fear,
That sent to thy pure eyes the sudden tear ?
Then, when thou saw'st him playing in the ring,
He would be first of all, he would be king,
To lash the whirling boxwood in thy hall,
From boyish throng to snatch the bounding ball,
Or snare the fluttering sparrows.   When he spoke,
How sweetly on his lips the Latin broke !

The Life of S. Augustine

How clear the thought ; how vivid was the wit
Kindling the fuel memory lent to it,
E'en in his playful words ; and what a flame
Of passion when they called him to declaim !
Most he of all within the vestibule,
The solemn awning, and the clamorous school,
Brings treasures back which parents' cost repay
And spur him fast and faster on the way.
What if, a fierier Tully, from the bar
He mount some day the throne proconsular ?

So, for one moment, spoke a mother's pride.
But how shall these with holier hopes abide ?
Within that very schoolroom, thou couldst know
Half the dark secret of thy coming woe.
These rhapsodies unlocked with toilsome art
Polish the tongue, but poison all the heart.
The ferule for the laggard to explore
The sinful meanings of their mythic lore,
Where taste, pronouncing all without a flaw,
Guards grammar rules, not Sinai's broken law !

5

Yes; listen there, and thou wouldst wonder less
That vain thy pleadings were for soberness ;
To him, though God was speaking in thee then,
They seemed the words of women, not of men :
Seemed,* with the spice and cinnamon at hand,
Fantastic echoes from a shadowy land.

Three years are gone : and what hath Carthage
     done
For that bright being given thee for a son ?
Long hast thou prayed and hoped ; thou hadst the
     dream
Of all the choicest flowers of academe
Showered on the loved one, which doth still deceive
The Christian mothers ; still they wake to grieve
E'en in a land where each time-beaten stone
For ages breathes of Christ, and Christ alone.
But did no Baal haunt the tawny light
Of columns basking on huge Bursa's height ?
On the hushed sand did then no scenic sin
From youth transported daily plaudits win ?

* " Confessions," ii. 3.

Away ! he'll find to righteousness the call
Where the rolled purple on the stage shall fall,
Where with heart melting and with streaming eye
He learns the love that bade Elissa die.
Shame, fictive tears ! are ye than hate more kind ?
Ye drain the succouring forces of the mind ;
Fit lesson here in pity more divine,
As One did pity in far Palestine :
Fit moments, in this caldron of desire,
To tread Christ's path, and trim the vestal fire.

And rhetoric lends her deadliest weapons now,
And all her guerdon garlands crown his brow,
And still, to flatter all his proudest hope,
Star-gazers spell his manhood's horoscope :
Or, from the embraces of an earthly love,
If once with longing true he looks above,
He sees in thought's sublimest solitude
Only its mirage of the Chiefest Good.

How to that sophist mind, those dazzled eyes,
Dimmed are the Scripture's sober mysteries !

The outlines of the God-Man melt and part
In the false splendours taken to his heart.
Ill brooks he now that tenderness should fill
The hour he gazes on a sunset hill,
And thinks, beyond it, of one shrine of prayer,
With one meek form for ever prostrate there,
On sand besprinkled with her constant tears;
And of a Master, too, who daily hears.

He cannot take that Master; cannot be
The slave of one who wore humanity.
Hark! what new jargon, and what haughty tones
Come to confuse Thagaste's simple ones:
" Our soul, which seems to sin, is still a spark
From God's own fire entangled in the dark;
The hosts of evil in the eternal fray
Have trapped it in foul tenements of clay;
But his corporeal brightness cannot sin,
While all those evil agents live within;
Fated to fly, and in the elect most soon,
Back to its central source in sun and moon.

No, this ye find not in your garbled word ;
Ye know not yet the Spirit of the Lord.
Were all His gifts at Pentecost to end ?
Lo ! on the Persian they e'en now descend !"
The youth he loved is on the bed of death,
But words are weak against Faith's parting breath.
He starts amazed ; Augustine shall not scorn
The dew that glistens on a soul new-born ;
But learn, amidst his grief's wild luxury,
His Jonathan doth live, himself doth die.

Back to the world, Augustine ; it is thine ;
For twelve more brilliant years thou there shalt
    shine.
Take there thy powers, thine understanding heart
Which grasps each science, and wins every art :
Take all the treasures of thy Father's store ;
Spend all on Fame, till thou shalt hunger sore ;
But leave, ah ! leave Christ's little ones to rest
By temptress tongue unharassed in their nest ;
For there a food divine lends love's strong wings,
Which lift not thee in all thy wanderings.

And now fair Milan's palaces among
He walks where statesmen meet, and soldiers throng.
Down each proud street the patriot eye may see
All the green ocean of her plains still free ;
Still with their cloudlike lines of lifted snow
The aerial Alpine ramparts stop the foe.
But whispers from another world are there
When blessèd Ambrose fills the Christian chair.
From clamorous tasks to please an emperor's ear
The Afric catechumen steals to hear :
And now how grandly after Arian storm
The Faith he once maligned is gathering form !
How the faint outlines which Plotinus drew
In John's great gospel glow with colours true !
" The Word descending to its fleshly screen
Sinks wounded on the way of life's dark scene ;
And the proud pilgrims of eternity,
Ceasing to trace their lineage in the sky,
Must lower their eyes where He is at their feet,
Must kneel abased and there a brother greet ;
And uncomplaining take his proffered cup :
Then, and then only, will He lift them up."

His proffered cup ?   What measure then for him ?
How deep must be *his* draught below the brim ?
To sell no more this power of life and death
That hangs in listening courts on pleaders' breath ;
To guide no longer to earth's dazzling goals
All the best powers of young impassioned souls ;
To lie no longer by a leman's side ;
To pass his coming wealth, and noble bride ?
Ah, strange to hear Faith's morning clarions sound,
Yet still in old sweet slumbers to be drowned.

Meanwhile in all earth's angels shall be seen
The rival sweetness of the Nazarene.
Yes, late and soon, O mother, seek the shrine ;
Still ever hunger for the food divine :
Let Music gushing from her freshest wells
Commend the truth in heavenly canticles ;
Let Continence usher through the awestruck crowd
Her lovely pomp of youth to Jesus vowed :
Let Antony, from Libyan solitudes,
Call in the hush of voiceless brotherhoods ;

And Victorine, the precious pearl to win,
Renounce his tongue's long triumph and its sin ;
Speak all !   Like arrows from the eternal bow
Ye lay in his pierced heart loose custom low.
Oh, when shall God's last wingèd word be spoken,
And the deep fountains of that heart be broken ?

It comes—the pathos of Pontinian's tale.
This giant wrestles with the heaven-sent gale.
See, with eyes flashing and with cheek aflame,
Deep in the garden glooms he hides his shame.
" And we, the wise, the learned, cannot prove,
As these have done, the violence of love !
Our brilliant wit this kingdom cannot win ;
And we stand still, while these are entering in !"
Ah ! follow not, Alypius : wait the end :
For heaven's own sign alone shall calm thy friend ;
Hark ! in a child's small voice he hears God speak,
And bid, on the dropped scroll, His answer seek ;
" Take up and read ;" oft through the whispering
        trees
Those words are wafted : and he hastes and sees :

Then peace, like ocean's floodtide, comes to fill
This halting purpose, and divided will:
No more from doubt can any anguish come;
His soul is anchored in a new-found home.

No need for vision now, or sign from heaven;
For in one moment every gift is given:
Sweetness, than pleasure sweeter comes; a light
Beats back the darkness of his mortal sight;
And love, still trembling with the loved One near,
Utters its joy untouched by any fear;
Yet, lest men's eyes should scan it, wills to wait;
Nor by one hour its freedom antedate.

     *   *   *   *   *

The tapers blaze around the laver's gloom,
Mute yet life-breathing as the Saviour's tomb;
And ere they pale before the paschal morn,
Deeds must be done, three Afric souls be born:
His, given by God, to God now given, the son;
His, friend of exile, dear companion;
His, who Truth's every treasure strong to seek,
By Ambrose waits now infinitely meek.

And Monica is there; her waking eyes
The dream of yore this night shall realize:
And that bright youth who smiled upon her tears
Stand on her Rule, and banish all her fears.
And, as he stands, what voices in the air
Climb and descend on Music's new-built stair?
Whose triumph-tones alternately prolong
Through the long aisles that ecstasy of song?
It matters not : but sure each singer caught
Notes that for aye to angel harps are taught.

Now, where they sit, his soul in equal flight
Can soar with hers beyond the star-sown height;
Thence, where love's flames serene for ever burn,
Hers but for one brief durance shall return :
Her ministries to husband, saint, and son
At Ostia end; her pilgrimage is done.
But thou, that graspest arms for earth's campaign,
Back to thy cities and thy sands again :
Soon shall yon vestal fires be burning low,
And Goths along the great Flaminian flow,

To climb with fire to Jove Capitoline :
Oh, then God's grander empire shall be thine ;
And thou shalt see, thy measuring reed shall trace,
Its laws, its bounds, its majesty of grace.
For grace redeeming only shall avail,
And all men's powers, by birth-sin tainted, fail.
Free and resistless as God's orient beams
Through His appointed sacraments it streams ;
And e'en from priestly hands that could betray
To His choice vessels wins an instant way,
And, whispering peace in hearts predestinate,
Yet awes them with His mysteries of fate,
Whose arm eternal still shall sift the crowd,
Lift up the humble, and abash the proud.

Yes ! thou shalt build new heavenly homes of rest
Amidst the smoking ruins of the West :
And thou shalt teach men for a thousand years
Truths told to thee amidst relentless tears ;
Thy heart's sad secret Heaven forbade thee keep,
And prodigals for aye shall read and weep.

So let the Vandal come ; his Arian horde
Shall never wrest from thee the Spirit's sword.
Thy dying hand shall wield it in the room
E'en where the tales of all his havoc come :
And while thy bishops gaze their mournful fill
On lips whose lifelong eloquence is still ;
Thine eyes are fixed where crimsoning sunset falls
On seven sad Psalms, thine armour on the walls ;
Where to the last their accents shall prolong
The godly sorrow which has made thee strong ;
In plight of friends thine efficacious prayer,
Thy safety sure, and victory, are there.

Paraphrase of Isaiah xxi. 1-10

A VOICE from the terrible land,
As sweeps o'er the burning sand
A whirlwind, and gathers the dust of the desert
 plains!
  I see! but grievous 'tis to tell
  The accents of a nation's knell;
"Barbarians come! the spoilers come! captivity
 and chains!
  Lo! Maday is round her,
  And Elam hath found her,
  There his armies are wending,
And all sighs have an ending."

What words are those ?   What rumours rang ?
They pierce me as a woman's pang ;
   My loins are filled with woe :
Mine ears are stunned with wild amaze ;
And Fear drifts darkness, as I gaze :
   My heart is panting low :
No more for me eve's lovely calm ! nought but a
  prophet's pains.

" For feasting open all the doors,
With carpets cover all the floors :"
   'Tis Babel's revelry.
But hark again !   " Arise, ye Lords !
Oil for the shield-belts ! whet the swords !
   Let battle end the day !"

For on the towers a watchman is set, on Zion's
  hill,
And by the Lord I ask, " What vision now is thine ?
Thine eyes are strained, they're drinking some wonder
  to the fill !"
" I see the conqueror come : I see the lengthening line.

From desert gloom
The asses come,
And camels there
Step pair by pair,
And side by side
The horsemen ride."

Sharply he listens, but in vain
They vanish on the hazy plain.
From his high station on the walls
His groan, as baffled lion's, falls ;
" I stand in the morning,
    I outstay the daylight,
Beneath the stars burning
    I watch out the night.
But hold ! again—'tis a cloud of men : I see them
    shine ;
        In line unending,
        Pairs of horsemen are wending.

" They shout of victory : they are calling,
' Babylon in the dust is falling,
    Her graven gods are low.
The sculptured forms of her high gods are prostrate
    now ! " "

Ah, for the flail that works the world ! and thee, my
    wheat,
Child that wast cradled on that floor, and livest yet,
I tell thee now this vision from the Lord.
Who rules those moving hosts, hath sent this Word.

In the Valley of Sia

UPWARD still the pines are marching,
  Sombre round their snow-piled lawns ;
Mounting where the eagle screeches,
  Climbing still the silver horns ;

Leaving many a cow-bell calling
  On the velvet slopes beneath,
And the noontide cloud-rifts dropping
  Golden gleams on purple heath ;

Leaving men and grass and cattle ;
  Kindred in a darkling throng,
Sons of other ages, singing
  All unheard eolian song ;

6

In the Valley of Sia

Where shall never shipmen's axes
    Lay their crests in ruin low ;
Never hunter tread their countless
    Needles on the virgin snow.

Nicolas ! see along the edges
    How they fringe the steep abyss
Spiring, some, for ever skyward,
    E'en upon the precipice.

Nurslings fallen in strangest cradles
    Well they knew, those seeds of fire,
Breeze may woo them, storms may buffet,
    Only sunward to aspire.

Nicolas ! Exile ! may such soaring
    To thy ardent soul be given !
Dare it droop in stony places ?
    Look it must still straight to heaven.

Take this memory of a noontide
  In the Pyrenean glen ;
Take it to thy Dacian cities,
  Bear it in the throng of men.

'To H.R.H. The

'December 14, 1891.'

AND so, like others of our time—
  Those good, glad days, eight years ago,
  With manhood's dawning light aglow,
And loud with careless laughter's chime—

You, sir, have found your heart's desire ;
  And now, with eager step elate,
  You enter through Love's palace-gate,
To tend his sacred altar-fire.

England rejoices !   Not alone
  In this bleak isle, mid northern seas,
  But wheresoe'er by vagrant breeze
The rumour of your spousal blown

Beyond our narrow, home-bound ken,
  O'er lonely lands 'neath alien stars,
  And late discovered harbour-bars,
Visits the hearths of Englishmen !

HENRY FRANCIS WILSON.
(Late Fellow of Trinity College, Cambridge.)

Duke of Clarence.'

A. d. xix. Kal. Jan. MDCCCXCII.

OLIM cohorti care sodalium,
Queis annus almos ille dabat dies
    Octavus abhinc et juventam
      Purpuream facilesque risus,

Tu nunc, quod istis cessit amantibus,
Voto potitus, limina trans dei
    Haud segnis incedes, beatasque
      Igne fovens adolebis aras.

Te prosequuntur cordibus Angliæ ;
Et ipsa nostrûm cui gelidis agri
    Undis inhorrescunt, et arctam
      Hancce supra levis aura si quam

Jam nuptiarum nuntia viserit,
Vastis relictas sideribus plagas,
    Portusque jam sero reclusos
      Sicubi deveniunt carinæ.